REAL
VAMPIRES

REAL VAMPIRES

Daniel Cohen

COBBLEHILL BOOKS
Dutton   New York

Library of Congress Cataloging-in-Publication Data
Cohen, Daniel, date
Real vampires / Daniel Cohen.
p. cm.
Includes bibliographical references.
ISBN 0-525-65189-6
1. Vampires—Juvenile literature. [1. Vampires.] I. Title.
GR830.V3C64 1995
398.21—dc20 94-22028 CIP AC

Published in the United States by Cobblehill Books,
an affiliate of Dutton Children's Books,
a division of Penguin Books USA Inc.,
375 Hudson Street, New York, New York 10014

Designed by Mina Greenstein
Printed in the United States of America
First Edition 10 9 8 7 6 5 4 3 2

To GEORGE and JUNE O'NEIL
—and their ancestors

CONTENTS

REAL
VAMPIRES

The Eternal Vampire

Of all the creatures that haunt our imaginations and trouble our dreams, the vampire is the greatest and the most persistent. Nothing else even comes close.

Every year, it seems, there is at least one big-budget, major vampire film and a half dozen or so minor ones. The racks of paperback books are filled with vampire novels which range from trashy potboilers to the lyrical and literary. The supernatural soap opera *Dark Shadows* featured Barnabas Collins, a vampire hero-villain. The series has long been off the air, but it has attained cult status through reruns and the sale of videotapes. Children's books and children's television often feature cuddly, nonthreatening vampires. At Halloween, capes and plastic fangs are perennial favorites. There are even vampire research societies (of varying degrees of seriousness) and vampire fan clubs.

In a sense, we really can't escape the vampire. And it would seem we really don't want to.

Surprisingly, the fictional vampire is a fairly late development, at least in English. The first great vampire story in English was called, appropriately enough, *The Vampyre* by John Polidori. It appeared in London's *New Monthly Magazine* in April 1819. It was popular primarily because its author was originally believed, incorrectly, to be the famous poet, Lord Byron. Bram Stoker's *Dracula*, which set the standard for all the vampire literature that was to follow, wasn't published until 1897. It has remained in print ever since and is unquestionably the most celebrated and influential supernatural novel ever written.

Yet in 1914, when Dudley Wright compiled the first serious study of vampirism in the English language, he said: "The subject of vampirism does not appear to have attracted litterateurs greatly . . . Among modern authors, Mr. Bram Stoker has made the vampire the foundation of his exciting romance *Dracula*, and Mr. Reginald Hodder has written a romance entitled *The Vampire* . . . Mention of these works almost exhausts the references upon the subject." Wright was wrong even in 1914, and to express such a sentiment today would be, well, unthinkable. But the point is made, that the fictional vampire is a comparatively recent development. The "real" vampire is not. He and she have been around for centuries. In the twelfth century, England seemed to have been afflicted by a plague of vampires. A century ago fear of vampires led people in parts of the United States to dig up graves and mutilate corpses. Even today rumors of vampires can create a great deal of excitement and generate genuine terror.

This is a book about "real vampires," not the vampires of stories or films, but vampires that people really believed in, and really feared.

First, let's define our subject. What is a vampire? Most of you will probably say it's a dead guy with fangs who gets out of his coffin at night, turns into a bat and sucks people's blood. But that is the vampire of fiction. The subject of real vampires is much broader than that.

Indeed, the subject is so broad that we have to limit it. The vampires in this book must have several characteristics in common. They must be dead or, to be more accurate, undead. They must be animated corpses, not ghosts or spirits. They must also attack the living. Though bloodsucking is a common theme, it is not absolutely necessary. Real vampires have also been known to devour the living or to cause deadly diseases. They don't have to turn into bats; in fact, the bat is a fairly late entry into the lore of the vampire. If vampires turned into anything, it was more likely to be a wolf.

A belief in vampires, or vampirelike creatures is both very old and very widespread. There is, for example, the story of Lilith, who in some ancient Jewish legends was the first woman on earth and Adam's first wife. But somehow she was transformed into a night-roaming monster that sucked the blood of newborn children. In the mythology of the ancient Greeks there is a similar creature called Lamia, who was once human and had been driven mad and kills her own children. She then is transformed into a creature that flies through the night killing as many children as she can by drinking their blood or devouring their flesh. For centuries, the cradles of newborn infants were hung with charms to protect them from Lilith or Lamia. Any unexplained death (and there were plenty of them) would be attributed to these vampire spirits. But while these creatures, and scores of others like them, were genuinely feared, they are not vampires, not for the purposes of this book anyway. They are evil spirits or ghosts, not moving corpses.

There are many stories, some quite modern, about living people who are compelled to commit crimes because of a "lust" or "need" for blood. Such criminals are often labeled "vampires" by the press. There is also a small number of noncriminals, who say that they are vampires, because they need or desire human blood. Such individuals are not vampires, they are just sick.

Occultists—those who believe that the world is controlled by strange, hidden, and often magical forces, have talked of "psychic vampires." These are individuals who are somehow or other able to suck the "life force" out of people they meet. But that is all too vague.

The vampires you are about to meet in these pages are not in any way vague. They are very solid and very dangerous.

Since the book *Dracula* and all the other works it has inspired so dominate the vampire scene, a lot of people have come to believe that there was a "real" Count Dracula. Well, there was a "real" Dracula all right, but he wasn't a vampire, and nobody believed he was. When Bram Stoker sat down to write his novel *Dracula*, he based his main character in part on Vald Tepes, a fifteenth-century Transylvanian prince who was also known as Dracula—which meant dragon or devil.

The historical Dracula lived in a violent and cruel era. But he was even more violent and crueler than his contemporaries. Some have regarded the historical Dracula as a national hero—he successfully fought off the Turkish invaders. Yet he was so ferocious that most regarded him as a villain, even a monster. For centuries he has been portrayed as an evil character in European plays, poems, and other works. However, before Bram Stoker, no one had ever portrayed him as a vampire. Vampire traditions were strong in Transylvania, but until the late nineteenth-century English writer appropriated Dracula's name and some of the details of his life, none of these traditions had ever been attached to him. So you see what I mean when I say there was a "real" Dracula, but he was not a vampire. That's why the Dracula story will not be retold in this book.

No, all of the vampires you will encounter in these pages are quite real—that is, they were really believed to be vampires, they were not some literary creation.

And I will begin with an account of my visit to a friend during which I discovered that vampires can be very close to home.

1

A Vampire in the Family

"And that," said my host, pointing to a small portrait on the wall, "is the family vampire." I was startled. It was not the sort of comment I had been expecting. I was not visiting a medieval castle in Transylvania. I was sitting in the living room of a fairly modern house in Rhode Island.

The painting, which appeared to be about a century old, was apparently done by a local artist of modest ability. It showed a plain, and simply dressed, young woman. There was nothing particularly striking about it. There must be thousands of similar portraits scattered throughout New England.

Though my interest in the bizarre and supernatural is well known, I had not expected to talk about vampires or anything like that. My wife and I had come to Rhode Island to talk about dogs. The people we were visiting raise champion Clumber Spaniels, a rare but engaging breed to which we are very much devoted. We had come to discuss plans for the annual Clumber Spaniel show. And yet, as has happened so often, the subject of the supernatural came up.

At first I suspected that my host might be kidding me. He has a deadpan, Yankee sense of humor. So I was wary. I didn't want to become the butt of one of his jokes. But I soon realized this was no joke.

My host produced a battered scrapbook that was pasted full of yellowed newspaper clippings from Rhode Island newspapers of the late nineteenth century. The collection seemed random. One from the town of Exeter told how the Hon. Z.H. Gardner of Exeter and his brother, Robert Gardner of San Francisco, "Made a tour of Washington and returned home last week. Mr. G. went through the White House and went into the room where President Garfield was sick, and he had some mementoes given him which he brought home."

Another article described an investigation of conditions at the town poor farm. One of the inmates at the farm was "William R. Slocum, an elder in religious appearance, [is] a man who was arrested some years ago for baptizing his calf and domestic animals . . ." He said that he was well treated at the farm. The reporter also talked to "The foolish woman in the yard. . . . She gobbled out a lot of words to the reporter about the woodpile, among which the words 'I done it' were distinguished." There was even a brief article on how cigarette smoking caused deafness. "Chewing is much less liable to cause these troubles than smoking," said this medical report.

But it was the vampire stories that were of interest to me. The longest of them was headlined:

THE VAMPIRE THEORY
That Search for the Spectral Ghoul in
the Exeter Graves
Not a Rhode Island Tradition but Settled Here

The story begins:

" 'Ugh!' says the person of refinement. 'Horrible!' ejaculates even the reader of the horrible daily papers. But those who believe in it express themselves thus: 'It may be true.' 'You may find one there.' 'I always heard it was so,' and 'My father and grandfather always said so.' From traditions of the vampire it is, on the whole, pleasant to be free, but how singular that this old belief of the Hindoos and Danubian peoples should survive in Rhode Island! Had such a superstition been acted upon in White Russia or lower Hungary, Rhode Islanders would have read it as fiction, or a strange, wild falsehood, but this exhumation in the South County, in the town of Exeter, with the names of the persons authorizing it known in the county, and with a modern physician assisting, is a fact divested of mystery or fictional description. People who believed in the theory went to the Medical Examiner of the District, and he had the bodies exhumed, and examined them. It is probable that this theory was never practiced in this State under a better light of publicity, discussion and criticism."

The article then goes on to tell the story of the family of George T. Brown, a local farmer. "The family had within four years suffered the loss of the wife and mother, four years ago; a daughter, Olive B., three years later, and Mercy Lena, another daughter, during the past winter." They had all died of consumption, what people once called the disease tuberculosis. Now a son, Edwin A. Brown, had come down with a particularly virulent form of the disease.

Though George Brown himself professed not to believe in vampires, some of his friends and neighbors were convinced that the only way that son Edwin's life could be saved "was to have the bodies of the mother and the two daughters exhumed in order to ascertain if the heart of any of the bodies contained blood, as these friends were fully convinced that if such were the case the dead body was living on the living tissue and blood of Edwin."

The local medical examiner, Dr. Harold Metcalf, declared such a belief to be "absurd." Nevertheless, the following Wednesday the doctor went to Shrub Hill Cemetery and unearthed the remains of the three women. Of the corpse of the mother who had been buried for four years, it was reported, "Some of the muscles and flesh still existed in a mummified state, but there were no signs of blood in the heart." The body of the first daughter, Olive, was then taken out of the grave, but only a skeleton, with a thick growth of hair, remained.

"Finally the body of Lena, the second daughter, was removed from the tomb, where it had been placed till spring. The body was in a fairly well-preserved state. It had been buried two months." The heart and liver were removed. The heart was clotted with blood. The doctor said that this was normal at that stage of decomposition. Nevertheless, "These two organs were removed, and a fire being kindled in the cemetery, they were reduced to ashes."

According to another published account in the scrapbook, "When the doctor removed the heart and liver from the body, a quantity of blood dripped therefrom . . ."

It was a picture of Mercy Lena Brown, whose heart and liver were burned because some people thought she had become a vampire, which hung upon the wall.

The end of this story was found in a clipping pasted near the back of the scrapbook:

THE THEORY FAILED
EDWIN A. BROWN OF EXETER DIED ON TUESDAY

The Removal of the Heart and Liver of His Dead Sister Did Not Cure Him of Consumption— Some Persons Still Credulous.

"Edwin A. Brown of Exeter died of consumption on Tuesday. This is the young man for the preservation of whose life the body of a dead sister was exhumed in Shrub Hill Cemetery some two months ago, and the heart and liver burned. The act was based on the belief that an evil spirit had retained its life within those organs by sapping the life from the sick brother."

The article went on to state that some people still insisted that the young man had been too far gone when the heart and liver were burned, but that the act would prevent others in the family from becoming ill in the same way.

Prior to this discovery that some of my friends had a presumed vampire in their family, I had read scattered references to vampire beliefs in America. For example, there is a brief item in a 1971 book entitled *True Vampires of History*, under the heading "Vampires of Rhode Island and Chicago."

William Rose, a citizen of the village of Placedale, Rhode Island, believed that his daughter was a vampire who was sapping away the vitality of the members of his family.

"With his own hands, Rose dug up the corpse of his daughter, cut out the heart, and burned the organ to ashes.

"The incident was reported in an 1894 edition of the *Providence Journal*.

"In 1875, a Dr. Dryer witnessed an occurrence

in Chicago, wherein a woman dead from consumption was disinterred and cremated as a vampire who preyed upon her living relatives, causing their deaths."

But the case of Mercy Lena Brown, which took place in 1891, was far and away the most completely documented account of vampire beliefs in America that I had ever seen and perhaps the best that exists. I was told that the author Bram Stoker had consulted articles on the case while he was doing his research for the novel *Dracula*, which was first published in 1897.

Vampire hunting in America was far more common than I had imagined. Far from being a rare and scattered event, it was a regular practice. One of the articles on the Mercy Lena Brown case contains a very extensive history of vampire beliefs, and indicates that what happened in Exeter was by no means an isolated incident.

"In all forms of the tradition the vampire left its abode and wrought its object at night. When the full moon shone and the sky was cloudless, its opportunity was supposed to be the most favorable. . . . Its active moments when wandering about were spent in sucking the blood of the living, and this was invariably the blood of some relation or friend of the dead. From this feeding, the body of the dead became fresh and rosy. . . .

"How the tradition got to Rhode Island and planted itself firmly here, cannot be said. It was in existence in Connecticut and Maine 50 and 100 years ago, and the people in the South County say they got it from their ancestors as far back in some cases as the beginning of the 18th century."

Just in time for Halloween, 1993, Paul S. Sledzik, curator of the anatomical collection of the National Museum of Health and Medicine in Washington, said that he had found evidence of fairly extensive vampire killing rituals among eighteenth- and nineteenth-century New Englanders.

Dr. Sledzik told a reporter for the Associated Press that he had helped analyze corpses from a cemetery near Griswold, Connecticut, and found one that clearly bore the signs of a ritual mutilation. The corpse, found in a coffin bearing the initials "J.B.," was buried in the Walton family cemetery of Griswold, which had been accidentally disturbed in a construction project.

Upon examining J.B., it was obvious that the remains had been tampered with sometime after the body itself had decomposed. The skeleton had been rearranged into a familiar symbol of death. The long bones of the upper legs had been placed on the chest so as to form an X. The skull was then placed on top of them.

Dr. Sledzik was able to determine that J.B. had

been a victim of tuberculosis. He also had a hunched and crooked shoulder, a crippled leg, and missing front teeth. "In life, J.B. could have been a frightening figure," said Dr. Sledzik. Memories of his frightening appearance, and the manner of his death, could have prompted relatives to make sure that he was still dead by piling his leg bones and skull atop one another.

Dr. Sledzik said that other researchers have also reported finding mutilated bodies from that era.

"When someone died of consumption, it was believed they could come back from the dead and drain the life of their living relatives," Dr. Sledzik said. "In order to stop this, family members would go to the grave and somehow attempt to kill the person again. If there was still flesh, they would remove it and burn it. Or they would remove the head. In the American tradition, just causing some disruption to the body was the way to kill a vampire." Driving a pointed wooden stake through the heart of the vampire, the method made famous in countless vampire stories and films, was more of a European than an American tradition.

According to Dr. Sledzik, the effects of tuberculosis on the bodies of its victims, when viewed with imagination, supported the folklore beliefs in vampires.

"Consumption is a very physical disease. People can actually see the person wasting away." But consumptives would also have great bursts of energy, he said. "So it made sense to people then that after death this desire for life would continue and the dead would be able to drain the life force from their relatives."

Dr. Sledzik concluded that people who saw their loved ones wasting away from consumption "felt they had to go into the graves and do something to stop the process."

That is clearly what happened in Rhode Island a little over a century ago to Mercy Lena Brown.

So it seems that vampires, or at least belief in them, is not limited to Central European peasants or other people who lived long ago and far away. It is a belief that is as American as apple pie.

2

Bitten by Dead Uncle Boris

When you hear the word "vampire," what sort of image comes to mind? It's probably someone elegant, wearing evening clothes and a cape. The vampire is mysterious, aloof, and compelling. This picture is, of course, based on the vampires of fiction.

Here is a description of Lord Ruthven, the first great vampire of modern literature, from John Polidori's 1819 novel, *The Vampyre*:

"... there appeared at the various parties of the leaders of the town a nobleman, more remarkable for his singularities than his rank. He gazed upon the mirth around him, as if he could not participate therein. . . . Those who felt this sensation of awe, could not explain whence it arose: some attributed it to the dead grey eye, which fixing upon the object's face, did not seem to penetrate . . . but fell upon the cheek with a leaden ray that weighted upon the skin it could not pass. His peculiarities caused him to be invited to every house; all wished to see him . . ."

The image of a vampire that we carry in our minds comes mainly from *Dracula*, not so much from Bram Stoker's 1897 book, but from the 1931 film starring Bela Lugosi. It was Lugosi who created the formally dressed Count with the heavy accent: "Goood Even-ing."

Stoker's original Dracula was somewhat more exotic looking, and he spoke better English. Here is how he is first described in the book: "Within, stood a tall old man, clean shaven save for a long white moustache, and clad in black from head to foot without a single speck of colour about him . . . The old man motioned me in with his right hand with a courtly gesture, saying in excellent English, but with a strange intonation:—

" 'Welcome to my house!' . . ."

The vampires of the extremely popular Ann Rice novels, like *Interview with a Vampire* and *The Vampire Lestat*, are beautiful, glamorous, sophisticated and by no means entirely evil. They are really attractive and sympathetic characters. They are about as far from the "real vampires," that is, the vampires that people really believed in, as you can get. The author acknowledges this in her first book, *Interview with a Vampire*. Two of her elegant modern vampires go in search of their roots. They visit the "old country." For vampires that is Central Europe. Transylvania, home of Count Dracula, fiction's most famous vampire, is part of the country of Romania. The whole region is steeped in vampire lore.

When Ann Rice's sensitive and well-dressed vampires get to their traditional homeland they are disgusted by what they find. The vampires there are not aristocrats in cape and evening dress. They are mindless monsters who wander the countryside in stinking and rotting clothes, killing their peasant relatives and neighbors. The villagers are able to keep them at bay through use of the traditional sharpened stakes and garlic. Author Rice glosses over reasons for the difference between the modern and traditional vampire.

The traditional Central European vampire, the

vampire that people really believed in, was most likely to be a dead peasant, whose hideous half-decayed corpse crawled out of the grave to kill, either by sucking their blood or other means, his family and former neighbors. Someone once described being bitten by a real vampire as being about as romantic as being bitten by your dead Uncle Boris.

Here, from the "old country," the homeland of the vampire, are accounts of "real" vampires.

From the village of Blau, in what is now the eastern part of Germany, comes this early eighteenth-century description of what must be regarded as one of history's toughest vampires.

In life this vampire had been a herdsman. Shortly after his death, he appeared in the houses of several of his neighbors. Within a week they were all dead. The people of the village decided that they could tolerate no more deaths. So they dug up the herdsman's body and drove a stake through his heart. It didn't work. The vampire awoke and laughed. He thanked the villagers for giving him a weapon with which he could fight off the dogs. That night he pulled the stake from his own heart and went on a rampage throughout the village, spreading more horror and death.

The villagers decided to call in a professional. The public executioner was sent for. He was instructed to dig up the body and burn it somewhere outside of town. As the corpse was being moved, it twisted around and made horrible noises, "like a madman." Just to hold it in place the executioner drove another stake through its heart. The vampire screamed, and blood flowed from the wound. Finally, the body was taken far enough away from town where a huge fire was built. After it was completely consumed, the village was troubled no more.

There was a very rich man who owned a mill. He had many servants working for him. Each night it was the job of one of the servants to guard the mill. But one by one these servants began disappearing. Morning would come and the night watchman was gone, and was never heard from again. Soon no one in the district would work for the mill owner.

The owner grew desperate for help. Finally, he found one young man who said that he was willing to guard the mill at night, if the owner would pay "as much as a man's head is worth." Those apparently were pretty stiff terms, but the owner finally agreed. And so the new servant prepared to spend his first night in the mill.

The young man didn't really believe in vampires. He thought that some human intruders were causing the trouble. He put a wooden trunk in the bed where he was supposed to sleep, and covered it with a blanket so that it would look like a sleeping man. Then he hid up in the attic to see what would happen.

He didn't have long to wait. The vampire, "wearing a long beard like a clergyman," came in and approached the bed. But when the vampire discovered that the "man" in the bed was only a trunk, he cried, "How hungry I am, and how hungry I must remain."

When the young man realized that the intruder was really a vampire he almost fainted, but he continued to hide until dawn was nearly breaking. Then the vampire left the mill. The young man followed the vampire and caught up with him, just as the sun was beginning to rise and the vampire was losing his powers. He then drove a nail through its forehead.

After that, he went back to tell his tale to the owner of the mill, but was so overcome by his story that, at the end of it he fell down dead. So he never collected his reward. But, then, neither did the vampire, for it never appeared in the district again.

In the year 1715, a soldier who was quartered in the house of a peasant on the frontier of Hungary witnessed a strange series of events. One evening he was sitting at the dinner table with his landlord when a stranger came in and sat down with them. The landlord and all of the others in the house were terrified, except the soldier, who did not have any idea as to what was going on.

The next day the peasant died. When the soldier asked about what had happened he was told that it was the peasant's father, who had been dead and buried for over ten years, who had come and sat down at the table. By this he had given notice to his son that he was about to die.

The soldier spread the story throughout his regiment, and it finally reached the ears of the officers, who decided to conduct an investigation. The Count of Cabreras, a captain in the regiment, was appointed to head the inquiry. The Count, attended by several other officers, a surgeon, and a notary, went to the house and took statements from the entire family. They all swore that the figure which appeared was that of the landlord's father and that everything the soldier had reported was completely true. All the other inhabitants of the village also attested to the same facts.

Here in the West, we would probably have attributed such a visitation to a ghost. But on the frontier of Hungary a vampire was immediately suspected. The body of the peasant's father was dug up and discovered to look as fresh as if it had just been buried the day before, though it had been in the grave for ten full years. The Count of Cabreras ordered that its head be cut off and that the corpse be buried again.

The Count then proceeded to take statements about other suspected vampires in the area, particularly about a man who had been dead for more than thirty years, and yet had appeared several times in his own home.

This one behaved in a more familiar vampire-like fashion. During his first visit he bit the neck of his brother and sucked his blood. The second time he appeared he treated one of his own children the same way. On his third visit he grabbed one of the family servants. All three had died within hours.

On the basis of this evidence the Count issued orders that the body should be dug up. Though it had been in the grave for thirty years, it was found to be fresh and undecayed. A large nail was driven through the skull, and the body was buried again.

A third person who had been dead for sixteen year was found guilty of murdering his two children by sucking their blood. He was dug up and his body was burned.

A report on this remarkable inquiry was sent to the court of the Emperor Charles VI, and the Emperor sent his own team of investigators, who confirmed all of the stories.

In September of 1725, in the Hungarian village of Kisilova, a sixty-two-year-old peasant died. Three days after the funeral he appeared before his son and asked him for food. His son gave him some food and he disappeared. The next day the son told his neighbors what had happened. That night the peasant did not appear, but the next night he came back and demanded food once again. No one knows whether the son gave it to him or not, but the next morning the son was found dead in his bed. Six or seven people in the village also fell ill that day and they died one after the other in a few days.

The governor of the district sent a report to the tribunal in Belgrade, and they sent two officials and an executioner to deal with the matter. The governor himself then went to Kisilova to see what happened. All the bodies that had been buried for the last six weeks were dug up. When they reached the body of the old man, they found that his eyes were open and of a red color. According to the report, he was found to be breathing normally though he was quite dead. From this they concluded that he undoubtedly was a vampire. The hangman drove a stake through his heart, and the body was burned. According to the report, "none of the marks of vampirism was found on the body of the son, nor on any of the others."

There is another celebrated vampire case from the same village, and the two accounts often are confused, though the details are quite different. In this case the vampire was a peasant named Peter Plogojowitz, who had died in 1728. Ten years later he appeared at night to nine people in the village. He began to choke them, and they all died within twenty-four hours. Plogojowitz's widow testified that she had also been visited by him since his death. His errand was to demand his shoes! That frightened the widow so badly that she moved to another village.

The inhabitants of Kisilova determined to dig up the body of Plogojowitz and burn it. But in order to do this they had to have the permission of the commander of the Emperor's troops in the district. The commanding officer had some scruples about granting permission, since digging up bodies was contrary to the religious practices of the day. But the peasants made it quite clear that if they were not permitted to dig up this accursed body, which they were fully convinced was a vampire, they would be forced to leave the village and settle elsewhere.

The officer was convinced that the peasants were serious and so he granted them permission to dig up the body, and himself went to witness what happened. When the corpse, which had been in the grave for ten years, was uncovered, it was "found to be perfectly sound, as if it had been alive, except that the tip of the nose was a little dry and withered. The beard and hair were grown fresh and a new set of nails had sprung up in the room of the old ones that had fallen off. Under the former skin, which looked pale and dead, there appeared a new one, of a natural fresh color; the hands and feet were as entire as if they belonged to a person in perfect health. They observed also that the mouth of the vampire was full of fresh blood, which the people were persuaded had been sucked by him from the persons he had killed."

At the sight of this, the people became more enraged than ever. They ran to get a sharp wooden stake which was driven into the heart of the corpse. Blood spurted out of the wound. The peasants then built a large pile of wood and burned the body to ashes.

In 1672, in the town of Kring, a man named George Grando died and was buried by Father George, a monk of St. Paul. But on returning to the widow's house after the funeral, Father George saw Grando sitting behind the door. The monk and the neighbors fled.

It was just the beginning. Soon rumors began to circulate of a dark figure being seen walking the streets at night, stopping now and then to tap at the door of a house, but never waiting for an answer. In a little while people began to die mysteriously in Kring, and it was noticed that the deaths occurred only in the houses at which the dark figure had tapped a signal. Grando's widow also complained that she was being tormented by the spirit of her husband, who night after night threw her into a deep sleep and then sucked her blood.

The chief magistrate of Kring decided to find out if Grando really was a vampire. According to the account, "He called together some of the neighbors, fortified them with a plentiful supply of spiritous liquor, and they sallied off with torches and a crucifix."

Grando's grave was opened and the body was found to be completely fresh. There was a pleasant smile on the corpse's lips and a rosy flush on the cheeks. At this sight the entire party was so terrified that they rushed back to town.

A second visit was made to the grave. This time there was a priest in the party. The villagers also carried a large sharp stake of hawthorn wood. The grave and the body were found to be exactly as they had been left. The priest knelt down, held a crucifix over the body and prayed. In a few moments great tears were seen rolling down the vampire's cheeks. The villagers tried to drive a stake through the heart of the corpse, but it just bounced off his chest. Then one of the group jumped into the grave and cut off the vampire's head. It gave a loud shriek and there was a convulsive contortion of the limbs.

A belief in vampires has remained strong in Central Europe well into the twentieth century. An account of "a terrible instance of superstition" was sent to a British paper from Budapest, Hungary, in February, 1912.

"A boy of fourteen died some days ago in a small village. A farmer, in whose employment the boy had been, thought that the ghost of the latter appeared to him every night. In order to put a stop to these supposed visitations, the farmer, accompanied by some friends, went to the cemetery one night, stuffed three pieces of garlic and three stones in the mouth, and thrust a stake through the corpse, fixing it to the ground. This was to deliver themselves from the evil spirit, as the credulous farmer and his friends stated when they were arrested."

An even more recent example of vampire beliefs was observed by Dr. Raymond T. McNally, an American scholar and expert on Central European folklore, particularly vampire tales.

"In 1969, I was passing through the village of Rodna, which is located near the Borgo Pass [that is where Bram Stoker located Castle Dracula]. Noticing a burial taking place in the village graveyard, I stopped to watch. As I talked with some of the bystanders, they told me that the deceased was a girl from the village who had recently died by suicide. The villagers were afraid that she would become a vampire after death. So they did what had to be done—and what I had read about for so many years. They plunged a stake through the heart of the corpse."

And finally there is a story that you may believe if you wish.

At the beginning of the eighteenth century, several vampire investigations were held at the instigation of the Bishop of Olmutz. This one took place in the Hungarian village of Liebava, which was particularly afflicted by vampires.

As the story was told, one night a villager hid on the top of the church tower. Just before midnight he saw a well-known vampire come out of his tomb. But he left his winding-sheet behind him before he went on his evil rounds. The villager came down from the tower, took the sheet and climbed back into the tower again.

When the vampire returned, he flew into a fury because he couldn't find his winding-sheet. The villager called to him and told him to come up to the tower and fetch the sheet. The vampire climbed the ladder, but just before he reached the top, the villager struck him a blow on the head which knocked him back down into the churchyard. The villager then climbed down, and cut off the vampire's head with a hatchet. From that point on, the village was never troubled by that particular vampire again.

3

The Peasant and the Vampire

Normally, vampires are a serious, a deadly serious, subject. But among the Russians, where vampire beliefs were strong, there are a lot of tales in which a clever muzhik, or peasant, outwits a rather stupid or absurdly boastful vampire.

One evening a muzhik was driving his cart filled with pots. It had been a long trip and his horse was very tired. The animal simply came to a stop alongside a graveyard and the muzhik could do nothing to move it. So he unharnessed the horse to let it rest and graze, and he decided to take a nap on one of the graves.

For some reason he was unable to fall asleep. He just lay there until suddenly he began to feel the earth under him move. He jumped to his feet and got out of the way. The grave opened. Out of it came a corpse, wrapped in a white shroud and holding a coffin lid. The corpse carried the coffin lid to the church and laid it at the door. Then it set off down the road toward the village.

This particular muzhik was a very bold fellow. He took the coffin lid back to his cart and waited there to see what would happen. He didn't have to wait long. Soon the dead man was back, and started looking for his coffin lid. But he couldn't find it by the church door. Then he saw the muzhik standing by the cart holding the coffin lid.

"Give me my lid," the dead man shouted. "If you don't, I'll tear you to bits!"

"And my hatchet—what about that?" answered the muzhik. "Why, it's I who'll be chopping you into small pieces!"

Suddenly the corpse became very polite. "Do give it back to me, good man. It is of no use to you."

"I'll give it to you when you tell me where

you've been and what you've done."

"Well," said the dead man, sounding a little embarrassed, "I've been to the village where I've killed a couple of youngsters."

"Well, then, tell me how they can be brought back to life."

The corpse hemmed and hawed a bit, but finally answered, "Cut off the bottom of the left side of my shroud. Take it with you, and when you come into the house where the youngsters were killed, pour some live coals into a pot and put the piece of the shroud in with them, and then lock the door. The lads will be revived by the smoke immediately."

The muzhik cut off the bottom of the left side of the shroud and gave the corpse back his coffin lid. The dead man headed for his grave. The grave began to open. Just as the dead man was getting into it, the cocks began to crow. The argument with the muzhik had delayed the corpse for so long that it was already morning and he did not have time to properly cover himself over again before the sun rose. One end of the coffin lid was still sticking out of the ground.

As it grew lighter the muzhik harnessed his horse and drove into the village. From one of the houses he heard loud cries and wailing. In he went, and there he saw two dead boys.

"Don't cry," he said. "I can bring them to life again."

"Do bring them to life, kinsman," said their relatives. "We'll give you half of all we possess."

The muzhik did everything the corpse had told him to do, and the lads came back to life. Their relatives were overjoyed. But they were also suspicious of the muzhik's apparent powers, so they seized him and tied him up. They said: "No, no, trickster! We'll hand you over to the authorities. Since you know how to bring them back to life, maybe it was you who killed them."

The muzhik protested, loudly and eloquently. Then he told them everything that had happened during the night. The story soon spread through the village. The whole population assembled and marched on the graveyard. They found the grave with a coffin lid sticking out of it. They dug it up and drove a sharp wooden stake right through the heart of the corpse to make sure that it would not rise from its grave to kill again.

The muzhik was rewarded handsomely and sent home with great honor.

Another popular Russian folktale concerns a soldier who escapes a couple of vampires, or vampirelike corpses, not by his cleverness but by sheer dumb luck.

One night a soldier, who had been given leave to go home to visit his parents, was walking along the road leading to his village. He passed a graveyard, and began to walk faster because he knew that graveyards were not safe during the night. As he walked he heard the sound of running footsteps behind him. Then a deep and terrible voice called out:

"Stop. You can't escape."

The soldier turned and saw that a corpse was running after him, gnashing its teeth. Naturally, he was terrified. He knew he couldn't outrun the thing and he looked for some way to escape. He spotted a little chapel nearby and ran to it. He hoped that in this house of God he would be safe from the monster.

The chapel was lighted only by two candles, and it took the soldier a moment to discover that he was not alone. There was another corpse laid out on a table. The soldier hid in the farthest and darkest corner of the chapel, fearing that the first corpse had followed him.

It had. The first corpse burst into the chapel and looked around wildly. At that, the second corpse jumped up off the table and shouted, "What have you come here for?"

"I've chased a soldier in here, and I'm going to eat him."

"Now, now, brother," said the second corpse. "He's run into my house. I shall eat him."

"I saw him first. He's mine!"

"No, he's mine!"

The two corpses became so angry that they began fighting. "The dust flew like anything. They'd have gone on fighting ever so much longer, only the cocks began to crow. Then both corpses fell lifeless to the ground and the soldier went on his way in peace saying 'Glory be to thee, O Lord, I am saved.' "

The power of religious symbols for warding off a vampire can be seen very clearly in another popular Russian tale.

One night a muzhik was driving his cart past a cemetery. A stranger dressed in a red shirt and a new jacket came up and asked for a ride. The muzhik didn't want to hang around the cemetery for long because it was supposed to be full of vampires. The muzhik, however, was an obliging fellow and did not feel it was right to leave the stranger in such a dangerous place. So he stopped his cart and the stranger climbed in.

The stranger said that he wanted to go to a village just down the road. When they reached the village they went to the first house. The stranger looked at the gate of the house and said, "Shut tight." This seemed odd to the muzhik, who saw that the gate was actually wide open. But the sign of the cross was branded upon the gatepost.

The same thing happened at the second house, and at the third. Finally, they got to the last house in the village. The gate was secured by a heavy chain and a huge lock. But there were no crosses. When the stranger looked at the gate the lock opened, the chain dropped off, and the gate swung wide.

The muzhik, who was now apparently under a spell, was told to drive up to the house. The stranger got out of the cart and told the muzhik to do likewise.

They went into the house, which was really little more than a rude cottage with simple furnishings. An old man and a boy were asleep on a bench. The stranger looked around and found a bucket in a corner. He took the bucket and placed it behind the boy's back, then he hit the boy on the back with his hand. Blood spurted out of the back and nearly filled the bucket. The stranger than drank the bucket of blood without a word. Then he turned to the old man and repeated the procedure.

After he was finished he looked at the muzhik and said, "It's getting light. Let's go to my place now."

In a twinkling the muzhik, his horse and cart, and the unpleasant stranger were back in the grave-yard again. The stranger reached out to grab the muzhik by the arm when the cocks began to crow and the stranger vanished. The muzhik went to the village where he told the authorities. They all went to the cottage at the end of the village where they found the old man and the boy dead.

This final Russian tale concerns an extraordinary vampire and his no less extraordinary opponent, a soldier.

This soldier had been given a leave to visit his home village. But it was quite a distance, and he had to walk. Along the way he passed the house of a miller, an old friend, and stopped in. The miller was delighted to see the soldier, and the two began talking and drinking, and didn't pay any at-tention to the time.

Finally, when it was quite dark the soldier got

up and announced that he was going to continue his journey to the village.

"Spend the night here, friend," pleaded the miller. "It's very late now, and you may run into trouble."

"How so?"

"A terrible magician has died among us, and by night he rises from his grave, wanders through the village, frightening everyone. How could you help being afraid of him?"

"Not a bit of it! A soldier is a man who belongs to the Crown, and Crown property cannot be drowned in water or burned in fire. I will be off. I am very anxious to see my people as soon as possible."

So off he went. The road led past a graveyard. Inside, the soldier saw a great fire blazing. He went to take a closer look, and saw the dead magician sitting near the fire repairing his boots.

"Hail, brother," shouted the soldier.

The surprised magician looked up and said, "What have you come here for?"

"Why I wanted to see what you were doing."

The magician threw his work aside and said to the soldier, "Come along, brother, let's go enjoy ourselves. There is a wedding going on in the village."

They went to the wedding and were treated with the utmost hospitality. The magician got very drunk and angry. He chased all the other guests out of the house. Then he put the newlyweds to sleep, took out two small bottles and a sharp needle. He pierced the hands of the bride and bridegroom with the needle and drew off some blood which he put into the bottles. Having done this, he said to the soldier, "Now, let's be off."

As they left, the soldier said, "Tell me, why did you take blood in those bottles?"

"Why, in order that the bride and bridegroom might die. Tomorrow morning no one will be able to wake them. I alone know how to bring them back to life."

"How is that managed?"

"The bride and bridegroom must have cuts made in their heels, and some of their blood must then be poured back into these wounds. I've got the bridegroom's blood stowed away in my right-hand pocket, and the bride's in my left."

The magician was feeling in a very expansive mood, and he began boasting. "Whatever I wish, that I can do."

"I suppose it's quite impossible to get the better of you," said the soldier, trying to sound as innocent as possible.

"Impossible? If anyone were to make a pyre of aspen boughs, a hundred loads of them, and were to burn me on that pyre, then he'd be able to get the better of me. Only he'd have to look sharp in burning me, for snakes and worms and different kinds of reptiles would creep out of my inside, and crows and magpies and jackdaws would come flying up. All these must be caught and flung on the pyre. If so much as a single maggot were to escape, then there'd be no help for it. In that maggot I should slip away."

The magician continued talking until they at last arrived at the grave.

"Well, brother," said the magician, "now I'll tear you to pieces, otherwise you would be telling everyone what I said."

"What are you talking about?" replied the soldier. "I serve God and the Empire."

The magician gnashed his teeth, howled and sprang at the soldier, who drew his sword and began to strike out furiously. They struggled and struggled and the soldier was almost exhausted. "Ah," he thought, "I'm a lost man, and all for nothing!" Suddenly the cocks began to crow, the sun started to rise and the magician fell lifeless to the ground.

The soldier took the jars of blood out of the

magician's pockets and went to the house where the wedding had taken place. He found the whole family in tears.

"I can bring your young people to life again. What will you give me if I do?"

"Take what you like, even were it half of what we have got."

The soldier then did as the magician had instructed, and brought the young people back to life. There was great rejoicing in the house where only moments earlier there had been weeping. The soldier was well rewarded. He then marched off to the mayor of the town and told him to call all the peasants together and to ready one hundred loads of aspen wood. They took the wood to the graveyard, and dug up the magician's grave.

The magician's body was placed on the pyre and set alight. As the corpse burned, it burst and out of it came snakes, worms, and all kinds of reptiles, and flying out of the flames were crows, magpies, and jackdaws. The peasants knocked them all down and flung them back into the fire, not allowing so much as a single maggot to creep away!

The body of the evil magician was thoroughly consumed. The soldier collected the ashes and scattered them to the winds. From that time forward there was peace in the village.

4

Chinese Vampires

The Chinese have beliefs very similar in many ways to the vampire traditions of Europe. In China, the creature is often called the *xiang shi*. The time between when an individual dies and when his or her body rots and turns to dust is considered one of extreme peril, for during that period the body may become inhabited by a *xiang shi*. This spirit lives inside the corpse and keeps it from decaying by preying on other fresh corpses or on the living. In most accounts the creature has "red staring eyes, huge sharp talons or crooked nails and its body is covered with greenish white hair."

Here are some of the many tales that have been

told for centuries in China of this or similar monsters.

Very late one evening four exhausted travelers arrived at an inn near the city of Shantung. The innkeeper said that there were no rooms available. But the travelers pleaded that they were much too tired to go on. Finally, the innkeeper agreed to put them up in a little shack some distance from the inn. The innkeeper failed to tell them that his daughter-in-law had recently died in that shack, and that her unburied corpse, stretched out on a plank, was just behind a curtain.

Three of the travelers fell asleep at once, but the fourth, sensing some unknown danger, remained awake. To his horror he saw a bony hand pull the curtain aside, and watched as the greenish, glowing-eyed corpse emerged. The creature bent down over the sleeping men one by one and breathed on them. The foul breath of such a monster causes instant death. When the creature approached the only traveler who was awake, he was almost paralyzed with fear. He held his breath while the thing bent over him and thus escaped the fate of his companions. When the monster had returned to its place behind the curtain, the man bolted for the door and ran out into the night.

His escape did not go unnoticed. The fleeing man could see the blazing eyes of the corpse behind him, and he could hear the approaching footsteps. He knew it was gaining on him. He ducked behind a huge willow tree to hide, and as he peered cautiously around the trunk of the tree he found himself staring directly into the burning eyes of the creature that was no more than a foot away. The thing let out a hideous shriek and made a leap toward him. That was just too much for the unfortunate traveler and he fell into a dead faint. In doing so he saved his life, for the corpse missed him and was plunged forward with such force that it hit the tree and buried its sharp talons deep into the wood.

The next morning the corpse, no longer animated, was found with its nails still stuck in the tree trunk. The intended victim was on the ground unconscious but alive. His three companions in the shack were dead, poisoned by the noxious breath of the corpse.

One night a man was walking down a lonely country road on a brilliantly moonlit night. Quite unexpectedly, he came upon a coffin that had been placed in the middle of the road.

He stepped back behind a tree and watched the coffin. To his horror, he saw the lid rise and a corpse climb out and walk away.

The man, of course, had heard of the *xiang shi* who left their graves to feed upon the living, and he was quite sure that he had just seen one of them. After he was convinced that the corpse had really gone, he filled the coffin with stones and pieces of broken pottery that he found along the side of the road. Then he looked for a safe place where he could observe what happened next. Nearby there was an empty farmhouse with a ladder that led to an attic. He climbed up and hid near a window through which he could watch the empty coffin that could be seen quite clearly in the moonlight.

Hours passed and nothing happened. Finally, he saw the corpse return carrying something. The corpse tried to climb back into its coffin, but found it full of debris. The man could see the corpse's eyes ablaze with anger. Its fury was so great that it was almost a physical presence, and the man became afraid. The corpse looked around wildly, trying to discover who had been tampering with its coffin. Then it spotted the farmhouse and the window and the man cowering behind it. It began to run toward the farmhouse. The man feared that his foolish bravado would cost him his life.

He was afraid to even look out the window. He heard the monster below shaking the ladder. But for some reason it seemed unable to climb up. It just stood on the ground rattling the ladder and shrieking. Then it threw the ladder down and disappeared.

Now the man was afraid that he was trapped. He gazed longingly at the ladder on the ground, but there was no way to get it back up. Then he noticed that there was a tree near the window. He climbed out of the window, jumped over to the tree, caught a branch and then made his way to the trunk of the tree and down onto the ground. He then started walking back to the road.

The vampire, however, had not gone far. It was simply waiting in the shadows, and as soon as it saw the man it began to chase him. The man ran as fast as he could, but he knew that he could not outrun a vampire. Just as he thought that all was lost, he saw a river. He knew that vampires could not cross running water. He headed directly for the water, plunged in and swam to the other side. When he looked back he saw the vampire standing on the far side of the stream screaming and gesturing wildly. Finally, it jumped up in the air three times, turned into a wolf, and ran off.

By now the dawn had broken, and the man knew the vampire's power was ended for another day. He once again crossed the river, and headed for the road. He had seen the vampire carrying something, and wanted to know what it was. There on the ground, next to the coffin, lay the body of a newly dead baby. The flesh had been half-eaten away and it had been sucked completely dry of blood.

There is a famous old Chinese tale about a vampire that seemed greedy, not so much for blood, but for money.

In the city of Nanking, the old southern capital of China, lived two good friends, Chang and Li. One day they discovered that both had to make a trip to the distant city of Canton. Since the journey was a long one, they decided to go together. After they reached Canton, Chang wound up his business quickly, while Li discovered that he would be delayed for a considerable time. Chang determined that he could not wait for his friend and that he would go home alone. Li gave him a letter to deliver to his family back in Nanking.

When Chang got back to Nanking, the first thing he did was to deliver the letter to the Li house. There he learned that Li's father had just died. Nevertheless, he gave the letter to the widow, extended his sympathies and performed the ritual offerings for the dead. By that time it was quite late, and Chang's own house was all the way on the other side of the city. The widow told him that he should have dinner and spend the night. Chang, who was very tired from his journey, quickly agreed.

Tired as he was, Chang found himself unable to sleep. Chang knew that the body of the old man was lying in a room just across the courtyard, but he was not bothered. Chang had no superstitious fear of the dead. But he did hear strange noises coming from the room across the courtyard. He arose and peered through a tear in the paper window. He saw Mrs. Li standing beside the bed on which her dead husband lay, holding an incense stick.

Poor woman, he thought. Then he heard her footsteps approaching his room. She stopped, and seemed to be doing something to the door. After a short time he heard her footsteps retreating. He tried to open the door, but it was locked. He did not know why.

Chang went back to the window and again looked through the tear. What he saw amazed and terrified him. The corpse sat straight up, and turned in his direction: "The face of the corpse was black, its eyes were hollow and glaring, and its whole appearance was fierce and horrible to behold."

The corpse jumped off the bed and made straight for Chang's room. It started pushing on the door, trying to get it. Chang pushed from the other side, but it was no use. The corpse battered the door down. Chang jumped behind a large clothes chest, just as the monster rushed in, and he turned the chest over on the creature. Then he fainted. When he awoke he found the widow Li bending over him, holding a cup of tea. The monster was nowhere to be seen.

As the puzzled Chang drank his tea, the widow explained what had happened during the night.

Her husband, old Mr. Li, she said, had been a very greedy and evil man. He would do anything to make money. It seemed that even death had not improved his character. He had come to her the night before Chang arrived and told her that Chang would come with a letter. He also said that Chang would be carrying a lot of money with him from the business that he had done in Canton. Old Mr. Li said that he was going to kill Chang and steal his money.

The widow had been distraught. She had gone to the room in which her husband's corpse had been placed and found that the body had returned there. She had prayed, to try and make him change his wicked plan, but the corpse had remained silent. She knew that she had failed.

That night, after Chang had gone to bed, she tried to block entrance to his room by tying the handles of the doors together. That was the noise that Chang had heard outside of his door. She had never expected that the dead man would be strong enough to actually break through the door. When he did, she was sure Chang would be killed, but the heavy chest had pinned the creature to the floor. Now it was daylight, and the corpse was quiet. She called the servants to put the corpse back into its coffin. She apologized to Chang and said she hoped that her husband's corpse would no longer bother anyone.

But Chang thought it was foolish to simply rely on hope. He was now convinced that old Mr. Li's corpse would become a menace unless his soul could be put to rest forever. He went to a nearby Buddhist monastery and talked to the abbot. Then a group of monks were sent to perform a service of exorcism over the body so that the soul of Mr. Li could be released. The body was then burned.

After that, neither Mrs. Li nor anyone else was ever bothered again.

A village in the mountainous province of Chihli was afflicted with a particularly vicious vampire. This creature spent the daylight hours in a cave above the village. At night it came down and killed and devoured villagers, particularly children. The desperate villagers sought the help of an aged and learned Taoist priest who lived nearby. The old man was finally persuaded to help them.

When he arrived at the village and surveyed the scene, he told the people that he had magical nets and snares which would keep the vampire from flying through the air. But he needed the aid of a fearless man who would actually enter the monster's cave.

He called for a volunteer. No one stepped forward. He said that without such aid, he was powerless to help them. Finally, one young man volunteered to help.

The priest set up an altar outside of the vampire's cave. He gave the young man two copper bells and told him that when the vampire came out of the cave, the young man was to rush inside and begin ringing the bells. He was to ring constantly, without stopping for a moment. This noise would prevent the vampire from returning to the cave. But if the ringing were to stop, even for an instant, the vampire would rush back into the cave and kill him.

As night approached, the villagers gathered around the cave at a safe distance. The young man crept to the edge of the cave. The priest stood at his altar making his incantations. As usual, as the last ray of the sun's light disappeared, the vampire came out of the cave. The young man rushed in and began ringing his bells.

"The vampire turned and glared at me with eyes like lightning, but could not seize me," the young man later explained. He continued to ring, and the vampire continued to glare, until "the first streak of dawn, when the vampire fell dead."

The villagers burned the creature's body, and were never troubled by vampires again. But from then on, the young man found that he could not stop making a bell-ringing motion with his hands. When people asked him why his wrists and hands moved constantly, as if he were ringing bells, he told them the story of the vampire that had ravaged his village, and how he had helped to kill it.

Two young men who were traveling together stopped to spend the night in a pavilion by a lake. The spot had a beautiful view of the water and the nearby mountains. They were awakened in the middle of the night by the sound of singing. They looked out to see the form of a beautiful woman standing by the lake. She was no ordinary woman, for she was wearing the clothes of a by-gone age.

"A ghost," said one of the young men.

"Ah," said the other. "If she is a ghost, she is a very pretty one." He called out to the woman outside the pavilion, "Why don't you come in?"

To his surprise, a woman's voice answered, "Why don't you come out?"

As happens so often in stories of this type, the two young men actually were foolish enough to go out into the darkness in search of the strange woman. At first, they saw no one. They called out. A voice answered. This time it seemed to be coming from the trees. They looked around, and suddenly they saw a woman's head hanging down from a nearby tree. They now knew what they faced was not an ordinary woman, not even a woman's ghost, but the far more dangerous vampire. They both screamed in terror and ran back toward the pavilion, with the head in hot pursuit.

They just made it back to the pavilion and were able to bar the door, when the head came crashing up against the door. The door held. The head then began gnawing at the wood. They could hear the wood splintering, and it would only be a matter of time before the head had chewed its way through. But then a cock crowed, and the first rays of the sun appeared on the lake. The head rolled down the slope and disappeared into the water. The young men were saved, but they never fully recovered from their terrifying experience.

A vampire head figures in one other Chinese tale. Two young men were walking near the Hsi Ch'ia lake. After walking for some time, they sat down for a rest. One of them had brought a jar of picked plums for a snack.

While they were eating the plums, they spotted a skull lying on the ground nearby. Feeling foolishly brave, they thought it would be very amusing to stuff the plum pits into the mouth of the skull. They did so, laughing, and then one of them asked the skull if the pits tasted salty.

They thought no more of the incident. But while strolling back home in the moonlight, they heard a noise behind them. They looked back and saw the skull rolling toward them calling out, "Salty, salty."

The two young men ran as if the devil were behind them, and in a sense it was. Finally, they reached a canal, where they were able to hail a boatman who took them aboard. As the boat drew away from the shore, they knew they were safe, for such creatures cannot cross running water.

East or West, there always seems to be an obsessive streak in the behavior of a vampire. They are compelled to perform a particular action. There is, for example, this ancient Chinese tale of a vampire who was compelled to paint.

In the city of Hangxou lived an artist named Liu I Shen. When his neighbor's father died, the son stopped by the artist's house on his way to buy a coffin, to ask Liu to paint a memorial portrait of the dead man. The artist gathered up his paints and set out for the house. When he arrived, the house was empty. All of the members of the family had left on various errands. But the door was open. Liu went into the house to look for the dead man who was to be honored with a portrait. He found the body laid out on a bed in a second-floor room.

The artist, who had done memorial portraits before, was not at all nervous about being alone in a house with a corpse. He just sat down and began to make a sketch. For a while he worked in silence. Then the dead man sat up and yawned.

Liu realized that the corpse had become a vampire. If he tried to run away, the vampire would attack. He thought that the safest course of action was to pretend not to notice. So Liu kept right on drawing. This was difficult, because the corpse mimicked every move the artist made, appearing to draw on imaginary paper just as Liu was drawing on real paper.

A short time later, the son returned. He had found the undertaker and arranged to have a coffin delivered. He went up to the second floor and entered the dead man's room. But when he saw his dead father sitting up and moving his hands, the shock was so great that the son fainted. The corpse didn't notice, and Liu pretended not to.

Soon after the son returned, a neighbor came by to help with the funeral arrangements. When he entered the dead man's room and saw the corpse sitting up, he too fainted. The vampire sat, and Liu sat, and both worked at their drawings, one in the air, the other on paper. The two who had fainted lay unconscious on the floor.

Finally, the workmen from the undertakers came, carrying the coffin. They entered the courtyard and began shouting to see if anyone was home. Liu decided it was time to act.

He called out to the man in the courtyard, "Quickly, quickly! Get some brooms and come up here as fast as you can."

The undertaker's men had encountered problems like this before, and knew exactly what to do. Two of them grabbed brooms in the kitchen area and rushed upstairs. As soon as they saw the corpse sitting upright, they began hitting it with brooms. The other two brought the coffin upstairs, and then all four grabbed the struggling corpse, stuffed it into the box and nailed the lid shut. Thus they put the vampire where it belonged. Only when they were finished was there time to go back to the kitchen and prepare tea to help revive the two unconscious men. Everyone praised the artist Liu for his cleverness and courage in dealing with the dead man who refused to stay quiet.

Jan Jacob Maria de Groot was a Dutch scholar who lived and traveled extensively in China during the late nineteenth and early twentieth centuries. He recorded another vampire tale concerning a man named Liu—quite a common name in China.

This Liu was a teacher who had come home for the holidays. He had to return to his post and told his wife to cook a meal for him early in the morning, so that he would be able to eat before his long journey.

The wife got up very early, washed some rice at the brook, picked some vegetables in the garden, and got everything ready. But her husband did not appear. She went into his room and called him, but there was no answer. She then drew back the curtains and found his headless corpse lying across the bed. There was not a trace of blood to be found.

The terror-stricken woman called her neighbors, and they called the local magistrate. Everyone suspected that the woman was somehow guilty of the murder of her husband, and she was thrown in jail.

Months passed, then a neighbor looking for wood saw a grave that apparently had been dug up. The coffin had been exposed, and he suspected grave robbers had been at work. He called others from the village, and they pried the lid off the coffin.

Inside was a corpse that had the features of a

human, but the body was covered with white hair. Between its arms it held the head of a man, which they recognized as that of Liu, the teacher. They reported what they had found to the magistrate, and he ordered that the head be taken away. But it was so firmly grasped by the corpse that the combined efforts of several men were not able to pull it away.

So the magistrate then told them to chop the arms off the corpse. Fresh blood gushed out of the wounds. But there was not a drop of blood in Liu's head. It had been sucked dry by the monster.

By order of the magistrate, the corpse was burned and the unfortunate woman was released from jail, with, one assumes, profuse apologies from the officials and her suspicious neighbors.

And finally, if ordinary vampires were not enough, the Chinese have a tale of a giant vampire.

There was a temple dedicated to the legendary heroes Kwan Yu, Liu Pie, and Chang Fei. But the temple had the reputation of being haunted. Even the priests would not stay there a moment longer than necessary. The temple was open only during the daytime, for the few days dedicated to the heroes in the spring and the autumn.

One night during the year 1741, a shepherd asked permission to sleep in the temple. His flock was to stay outside, under the temple porch.

The priests warned him that the temple was haunted. But the shepherd said he was not afraid. He had a candle to light his way, and a whip with which to protect himself. Once inside the temple, the shepherd was accompanied only by the statues of the three heroes. Yet he could not escape the feeling that there was something else there as well.

Around midnight, he was awakened by a noise coming from the pedestal beneath the statues. The shepherd turned toward the sound, and saw a giant with blazing eyes, great claws, and a greenish body covered with white hair. It smelled like a rotting corpse.

The giant attacked, but the shepherd avoided the slashing talons, and kept the monster at bay with his whip. He was able to get out of the temple alive.

The following day he told people what he had experienced. Then he returned to examine the pedestal from which the greenish monster had emerged. A mist and the terrible smell of decay seemed to arise from the cracked stone.

The shepherd reported all of this to the town magistrate, who gave his permission to dig up the pedestal. When the townspeople dug below the stone, they found the body of a giant man, dried like a mummy. It perfectly fit the description that had been given by the shepherd.

They built a huge funeral pyre next to the temple, and placed the giant corpse upon it. As the fire began to consume the monster, it screamed wildly, and blood poured from the burning carcass.

After that the temple was completely free from any disturbances.

The Undead of Old England

5

During the twelfth century, England seemed to be afflicted by a virtual epidemic of walking corpses. They weren't quite vampires, that is, they didn't drink blood, though many believed that they somehow lived off the blood of the living. They certainly weren't conventional ghosts. Nor were they zombies, brought back to a half-life by some magical spell. They were . . . well read on and decide for yourself.

Several of these accounts appear in an odd little book called *Courtiers' Trifles* written by Waler Map, a highly placed churchman. He was Archdeacon of Oxford in 1197, and held a number of other important clerical positions. The book appears to be a collection of anecdotes and observations that Map wrote during his lifetime. These fragments were probably collected in book form some years after his death, but they are undoubtedly his work.

In one of his accounts, Map wrote, "The most wonderful thing that I know happened in Wales. William Laudun, an English soldier, a man of great strength and proven courage, went to Gilbert Foliot, who was at the time Bishop of Hereford . . . and said to him, 'My lord, I come to thee to ask for counsel.' "

Foliot told the bishop that a certain Welshman, an evil and godless man, had recently died in his house. Four nights after the Welshman died, he returned and called out the names of several who lived in the house. "As soon as they are called by him, they sicken and within three days they die, so that now but a few are left."

The bishop was amazed and horrified by the story, and the fact that "the accused wretch is able to rouse himself and walk abroad in his dead body."

He suggested that the corpse be dug up, "and then do you cut through its neck, sprinkling both the body and the grave throughout with holy water, and so rebury it."

These instructions were followed to the letter, but the ceremony did not work. The dead man continued to return to torment and kill the living. "Now it happened that on a certain night, when only very few were left, William himself was called three times by name. But he, being bold and active and knowing who it was, suddenly rushed out, brandishing his drawn sword. The demon fled fast, but he pursued it to the very grave, and as it lay therein he clave its head through from the neck."

That seemed to do the trick. "At that very hour, the persecution they endured from this demonical wanderer ceased, and since that time neither William himself nor any one of the others has suffered any harm . . . We know that this thing is true, but the cause of the haunting remains unexplained."

Another story related by Map took place in the time of Roger, Bishop of Worcester. Another sinful and godless man died, but a few days after he was buried, he was seen wandering about the town. The people of the town, who were either braver or more foolish than most, followed the walking corpse around "until he was surrounded in an orchard by all the people of the neighborhood. And it was stated that he was seen there for three days."

But it was not considered to be a good idea for a corpse to be walking around, so Bishop Roger was consulted about the problem. He said that a cross should be put up over the man's grave, "and that the spirit should be laid. But when the demon had come to the grave, and a great crowd of people followed him, he leaped back in alarm—as we think, at the sight of the cross—and he fled elsewhere. Then the people, acting upon wise advice, removed the cross, and the demon rushed into the grave, covering himself with earth, and immediately after the cross was raised upon it again, so that he was laid there without causing any disturbance."

Similar stories appear in the history produced by William of Newburgh. While Map was always regarded as a storyteller and something of a gossip, William has been called "the father of historical criticism." Yet his stories are, if anything, even more sensational.

One of his accounts is headed: "Of the extraordinary happening when a dead man wandered abroad out of his grave." It was supposed to have taken place in 1196, and was told to William by Stephen, Archdeacon of the diocese in which the event occurred.

"A certain man" died and was decently buried.

But the night after the burial, he appeared in his wife's bedroom. He not only frightened her, but he jumped up and down on her, very nearly killing the poor woman. The next night the torment was repeated in exactly the same way.

On the third night, the woman decided that she must protect herself. She had a number of her friends gather in her bedroom and remain awake, so that they could drive off the attacker.

"Nevertheless, he visited her; but when he was driven away by the shouts and cries of those who were keeping watch, so that he could do her no harm, he swiftly departed. Having been thus baffled and repulsed by his wife, he proceeded in exactly the same manner to harass and annoy his brothers, who resided in the same town."

They adopted the same precautions used by their sister-in-law. They stayed awake all night, surrounded by the members of their household, everyone on guard, "and all ready to receive and repel the onset of the dead man." The dead man appeared, but the crowd of guardians discouraged him. "It seemed as though he were only wishful, or only had the power, to molest those who were asleep, and he was kept at bay by the vigilance and courage of any who were on their guard and waking."

But the dead man was not easily discouraged. He roamed the town, tormenting the animals and any of his former friends and neighbors whom he happened to find sleeping. "Accordingly, throughout the town in every house there were certain of the family who were kept awake and mounted guard all night long, whilst everybody was anxious and fearful lest they should be subjected to some sudden and unforeseen attack."

At first, the dead man came only at night. But then he began to wander about in broad daylight. He was "dreaded by all, although actually he was seen but by a few. Very often he would encounter a company of some half-a-dozen and he would be quite clearly discerned by but one or two of the number, although all of them very perceptibly felt his horrible presence."

The town's inhabitants, who were "well-nigh scared out of their senses," decided to seek help from the church. Their request was sent to the Bishop of Lincoln, who was "greatly amazed" at what he heard. He consulted with many learned churchmen "from whom he learned that similar occurrences had often taken place in England, and many well-known instances were quoted to him."

Everyone agreed that the only sure solution to the problem was to dig up the body and burn it.

But the bishop believed that such an act was contrary to church law. He had another plan. No one seemed to know what sins the dead man had committed that made it necessary for him to wander from his grave. So the bishop wrote a letter, absolving the dead man from whatever it was that caused him to leave his grave. The tomb was opened, "and the body was found therein uncorrupt, just as it had been laid upon the day of his burial." The letter of absolution was placed on his chest, and the tomb sealed again.

There is a happy ending. "The dead man never wandered abroad, nor had he the power to injure or frighten anybody from that very hour."

Another story related by William took place in the town of Berwick. Here a wealthy and respected man died. But after his death it was discovered that he had really been "a most infamous villain."

Shortly after he was buried, he left his grave, "to rush up and down the streets of the town, whilst the dogs howled and bayed in every direction what time this evil thing was abroad. Any citizen who chanced to meet him was distraught with terror, and then just before daybreak he returned to his grave."

The town was terrified, and very nearly paralyzed by these appearances. "Nobody dared to step outside his door after nightfall, so terribly did they all dread to meet this fatal monster."

The townsfolk met to decide what to do. People were afraid that, "if by some unlucky chance they met this living corpse, they would be fearfully assaulted and injured by the dead man." Others pointed to a more long-range danger. The walking corpse was rotting, and unless something was done quickly, "owing to the fact that black decomposition of this foul body horribly infected the air with poisonous pollution as it rushed to and fro, the plague or another fatal disease might break out and sweep away many."

So ten young men, known for their bravery, were chosen to dig up the corpse. They were then to hack it into small pieces and burn it. When this was done, calm reigned in the town, at least for a while. "But there very shortly broke out a terrible pestilence, which carried off the greater part of that town. And nowhere else did the plague rage so fiercely."

Another town, facing a similar problem, fared better. An unworthy man was mistakenly given a Christian burial, "which he did not deserve and which profited him nothing."

He wandered the streets at night, "whilst on every side the dogs were howling and yelping the whole night long."

But fear of meeting the dead man was only a

small part of the townsfolks' worry. "The air became foul and tainted as this fetid and corrupting body wandered abroad, so that a terrible plague broke out and there was hardly a house which did not mourn its dead, and presently the town, which but a little while before had been thickly populated, seemed to be well-nigh deserted, for those who survived the pestilence and these hideous attacks hastily removed themselves to other districts lest they also should perish."

The survivors met with the parish priest at his home to try and figure out what to do. But two young men, brothers who had lost their father in the epidemic, decided that the time for talk and planning was over. "The monster hath slain our father, and if we do not look about, he will before long slay us too. Let us, therefore, dare a bold deed which will provide for our safety and also avenge the murder of our dear father." Since all of the leading people of the town were at the meeting, there was no one to stop them. "Let us, therefore, exhume this foul pest and let us burn him to ashes with fire."

They armed themselves with sharp spades and went to the cemetery. They began to dig, but found they did not have to dig very far. The body was covered only with a thin layer of earth. "It was gorged and swollen with a frightful corpulence, and its face was florid and chubby, with huge, red puffed cheeks, and the shroud in which he had been wrapped was all soiled and torn. But the young men, who were mad with grief and anger, were not in any way frightened. They at once dealt the corpse a sharp blow with the keen edge of a spade, and immediately there gushed out such a stream of warm red gore that they realized this vampire had fattened with the blood of many poor folk."

They dragged the body outside of town and started a large fire. Then they went to the priest's house to tell others what they had done. Everyone rushed to the spot where the body was to be burnt, to witness the destruction of the monster.

"Now, no sooner had that infernal monster been thus destroyed than the plague, which had so sorely ravaged the people, entirely ceased, just as if the polluted air was cleansed by the fire which burned up the hellish brute who had infected the whole atmosphere."

William also recorded the story of a priest who could not be kept in his grave. This particular priest was not a particularly pious man. In fact, he was mockingly called the Dog Priest, because he was so addicted to hunting with horse and hounds.

Shortly after he was buried, the Dog Priest climbed out of his grave and began to bother the monks in the Abbey of Melrose where he had been buried. Four of the bravest and most pious monks were assigned to watch the grave.

By the time midnight struck, they were all very cold. So three of them went to a nearby lodge, where they could warm themselves. But their leader resolved not to give up his vigil. As soon as three of the guardians left, the monster awoke.

"When the monk saw the monster close at hand, realizing that he was all alone, he felt a thrill of horror; but in a moment his courage returned. He had no thought of flight, and as the horrible creature rushed at him with the most hideous yell, he firmly stood his ground, dealing it a terrific blow with a battle-ax which he held in his hand."

The dead man groaned when he was struck, and ran away. But the monk followed him and chased him back to his grave, which seemed to open on its own, and then close after the corpse jumped in. The following morning the grave was dug up. The corpse had a terrible wound in its back, where it had been struck by the battle-ax. The remains were carried outside of the monastery, where a huge fire was built. When the remains had been reduced to ashes, the ashes were scattered to the wind.

Said William, "I have related this story quite simply and in a straightforward manner, just as it was told to me by the monks themselves."

William was well aware that many would doubt such stories, "unless they were amply supported by many examples which have taken place in our own days, and by the unimpeachable testimony of responsible persons." He noted that he could find no such stories in old histories, "and we know that those writers were always eager to include in their chapters any extraordinary or wonderful event." But since such stories had become so common in the twelfth century that if he wrote out all of them that he had heard, "I suspect, it would become not a little wearisome to read."

6

The Vampire of Croglin Grange

You would not expect one of the most hair-raising vampire tales to come out of a book called *Memorials of a Quiet Life* published in 1871. Particularly if that book was written by a very respectable and responsible Victorian clergyman. But that's just where the celebrated tale of "The Vampire of Croglin Grange" is found.

The author of *A Quiet Life* was Dr. Augustus Hare, and he was not reporting a firsthand encounter, but what had been told to him by a man named Captain Fisher.

For hundreds of years, the Fisher family had

owned what is described as "a very curious place in Cumberland, which bears the weird name of Croglin Grange." The most curious feature of the house, it seems, was that, unlike other houses of that time and place, Croglin Grange was only one-story high, and thus rather small. But it had a terrace "from which large grounds sweep away towards the church in the hollow, and a fine distant view."

Eventually, the Fisher family grew too large for the house. Instead of adding another story, which was the custom, the family moved to a different house, and rented Croglin Grange.

It was not a house that would have suited everyone. It was too small for the customary large families of the time. And it was a rather isolated structure located in a remote rural district. But it seemed to suit the new tenants exactly. They were two brothers and a sister. They did not need a large house, and the isolation did not seem to bother them in the slightest. They quickly threw themselves into "all the little social pleasures of the district" and made themselves very popular. They passed their first winter in Croglin Grange quite happily.

The story of the vampire starts on an extremely hot day in the following summer. The sister spent most of the day sitting on the veranda, unable to work because of the intense sultriness of the summer day. The three tenants of Croglin Grange ate dinner on the veranda, and then sat out there to enjoy the cooler air that came up as the sun began to set. The moon rose over the belt of trees which separated the lawn of the Grange from the nearby churchyard.

When it finally came time to go to bed, "the sister felt that the heat was still so great that she could not sleep, and having fastened her window, she did not close the shutters—in that very quiet place it was not necessary—and propped against the pillows, she still watched the wonderful, the marvelous beauty of that summer night."

This tranquil scene was about to change in a most dramatic and horrible way. Gradually, the sister became aware of two lights flickering in and out of the belt of trees near the churchyard. As she looked, she saw that the two lights were "fixed in a dark substance, a definite ghastly *something*, which seemed every moment to become nearer, increasing in size and substance as it approached." The thing, whatever it was, was scuttling across the lawn and heading directly for the window of her room.

"She longed to get away, but the door was close

to the window, and the door was locked on the inside, and while she was unlocking it, she must be for an instant nearer to it. She longed to scream, but her voice seemed paralyzed, her tongue glued to the roof of her mouth."

Then, quite abruptly, the thing made a turn, as if it was no longer coming directly toward the window but going around the side of the house. At that moment the girl jumped out of bed, and rushed toward the door. But as she was frantically trying to unlock the door, she heard an ominous scratching upon the window. Turning, she got her first good look at the thing, and she wished that she hadn't. What she saw was "a hideous brown face with flaming eyes glaring in at her."

That sight was enough to drive her back into bed. The creature, however, continued to scratch at the window. "She felt a sort of mental comfort in the knowledge that the window was securely fastened on the inside. Suddenly, the scratching sound ceased, and a kind of pecking sound took its place. Then, in her agony, she became aware that the creature was unpicking the lead! For many years, panes of glass were secured in windows with lead solder. If the lead were removed, the pane of glass would simply fall out. And that's just what happened.

"The noise continued, and a diamond pane of glass fell into the room. Then a long bony finger of the creature came in and turned the handle of the window, and the window opened, and the creature came in."

What happened next sounds like a scene out of a cheap vampire novel. The girl was so terrified that she could not scream. The creature came over to the bed, "and it twisted its long bony finger into her hair, and it dragged her head over the side of the bed, and—it bit her violently in the throat."

The shock of the bite broke the hypnotic hold that the creature seemed to have exercised over her. And she screamed. That woke her brothers, who rushed to her room. But the door was locked on the inside. It took a moment for the brothers to find a poker and use it to force the door open. By the time they got into the room, the creature had run off. Apparently, it had escaped back through the window. They found their sister lying across the bed, unconscious and bleeding profusely from a wound in the throat.

"One brother pursued the creature, which fled before him through the moonlight with gigantic strides, and eventually seemed to disappear over the wall into the churchyard."

The girl had received a terrible shock, and she

had lost a lot of blood. But she had a strong constitution and was able to recover rapidly. She was also a tough-minded unromantic sort, not given to believing in vampires or other supernatural creatures. She was convinced that she had been attacked by a lunatic who had escaped from some asylum and found his way to Croglin Grange.

The girl seemed well enough, but the doctor who had been called in on the case recommended that she leave Croglin Grange for a while, and have a complete change of scenery. So her brothers took her to Switzerland.

For several months, she hiked in the mountains, painted watercolors, and generally did what British tourists of the time did when they visited Switzerland. But as autumn came on, the girl urged her brothers to return to Croglin Grange. "We have taken it," she said, "for seven years, and we have only been there one; and we shall always find it difficult to let a house which is only one-story high, so we had better return there; lunatics do not escape every day."

Her brothers readily agreed, and soon they were back in Croglin Grange. Since the house was quite small, there could not be any great change in living arrangements. The sister kept the same room. "But it was unnecessary to say she always closed the shutters, which, however, as in many old houses, always left one top pane of the window uncovered."

The brothers both moved into the room right next to hers, and they always kept loaded pistols in their room.

The winter was uneventful. Though it would be a mistake to say that the events of the past summer had been forgotten, they had at least been pushed to the back of the girl's mind, until one night in March. "The sister was suddenly awakened by a sound she remembered only too well—scratch, scratch, scratch upon the window, and looking up, she saw, climbed up to the topmost pane of the window, the same hideous brown shriveled face, with glaring eyes, looking at her."

This time she was not paralyzed by fear, and she began screaming immediately. Her brothers rushed out of their room, brandishing their pistols. The creature was already fleeing across the lawn. One of the brothers fired and hit it in the leg, but it continued to stumble and run forward at great speed. It scrambled over the wall into the churchyard, and seemed to disappear into an ancient burial vault.

"The next day the brothers summoned all the tenants of Croglin Grange, and in their presence the vault was opened. A horrible scene revealed itself. The vault was full of coffins; they had been broken open, and their contents, horribly mangled and distorted, were scattered over the floor. One coffin alone remained intact. Of that, the lid had been lifted, but still lay loose upon the coffin. They raised it, and there, brown, withered, shriveled, mummified, but quite entire, was the same hideous figure which had looked in at the windows of Croglin Grange, with the marks of a recent pistol shot in the leg: and they did the only thing that can lay a vampire—they burnt it."

That is the story of the vampire of Croglin Grange, as it was reported in a book published in 1871. It is reported by a respectable clergyman as a true story. But is it true? The case has been investigated by a number of people. Back in 1924, Charles G. Harper was unable to find any place in Cumberland named Croglin Grange. He did find a Croglin Low Hall and a Croglin High Hall, but both of these were two-story buildings, and the account was very specific about Croglin Grange having only one story. The nearest church to these buildings was at least a mile away, much too far away to be the church in the story, and that churchyard "contains no tomb which by any stretch of the imagination would be identified with that described" in the original account.

An American investigator, D. Scott Rogo, found some suspicious similarities between the story found in the Reverend Dr. Hare's book to the opening chapter of *Varney the Vampire or The Feast of Blood*. *Varney* was one of the first vampire novels written in English, and one of the earliest of a form of popular novels called "bloods" or "penny dreadfuls." They were sold in weekly installments that cost a penny. Penny dreadfuls had titles like *Wagner the Wehr-Wolf* and *The Skeleton Clutch*, or *The Goblet of Gore*. Despite its fame, no one really knows when *Varney* was written; somewhere around 1840 is the best guess. To make matters worse, no one is sure who wrote it. Opinions are divided as to whether the author was Thomas Peckett Prest, the "King of the Bloods," or the equally prolific James Malcolm Rymer, also known as "Merry Malcolm." These energetic fellows could be working on a dozen novels at a time and turn out sixty or seventy thousand words a week, an astonishing output. They rarely signed their work. And the prose style is truly dreadful.

Compare these excerpts from *Varney* to the account of the Vampire of Croglin Grange:

"A tall figure is standing on the ledge immediately outside the long window. It is its finger-nails upon the glass that produces the sound so like the hail, now that the hail has ceased. . . . A small pane of glass is broken, and the form from without introduces a gaunt hand, which seems utterly destitute of flesh. The fastening is removed, and one-half of the window, which opens like folding doors, is swung wide open upon its hinges.

"And yet now she could not scream—she could not move. . . . With a sudden rush that could not be foreseen . . . the figure seized the long tresses of her hair, and twining them round his bony hands he held her to the bed. . . . With a plunge he seizes her neck in his fang-like teeth—a gush of blood, and a hideous sucking noise follows."

This is the sort of prose that thrilled mid-Victorian workingmen and women. *Varney* went on, and on, for nearly nine hundred closely printed pages, until the book not so much ended, it simply collapsed with exhaustion.

Since *Varney* was published some thirty-five years before the Croglin Grange story, the similarities cannot be ignored or easily explained away.

Rogo concluded that Captain Fisher must have simply made up the story, basing it on *Varney the Vampire*, perhaps because he was trying to create a local tourist attraction. Haunted houses, or any place that has a supernatural association, have always had great appeal in Britain.

The explanation seemed compelling. But just a

few years after Rogo wrote his exposé, another investigator, F. Clive-Ross, visited the area where the vampire attack was supposed to have taken place. At the church he found this information in a printed history: "Croglin Low Hall is the ancient Manor House of Little Croglin. It belonged to the Dacre family until 1589. There was a second church in Croglin, probably serving as a private chapel to the house. Nothing of this church now exists. The house is now a farm." He also discovered that until the early eighteenth century, Croglin Low Hall was called Croglin Grange.

When he visited the house, he found that it was indeed two stories, but apparently it had been raised one story in about 1720. It had always been assumed that the Croglin Grange vampire story dated from the mid- to late nineteenth century. But local residents told Clive-Ross that the story is really much older, dating from sometime between 1680 and 1690. At that time, there would have been a one-story house called Croglin Grange next to a church. And it would all have happened long before *Varney the Vampire*. He also heard other stories of attacks by a vampire long ago.

Clive-Ross's investigation points to another explanation for the Croglin Grange story. Instead of being a mid-Victorian encounter, which is what everyone assumed, the story was really based on a much older account. When Captain Fisher retold the old story, he may have been influenced by the popular *Varney*. But the story of the Vampire of Croglin Grange did not come from a cheap vampire novel.

7

The College Vampire

Ronald Seth is a British author who has written extensively on the bizarre and the occult. One of the strangest stories he ever told was one that he had personally experienced or, to be more accurate, witnessed when he was a student at Cambridge University in the late 1920s.

One of his fellow students was named Peter Grimes; he was a classical scholar. Grimes had a splendid set of rooms in the college. But the rooms had some disadvantages. First, they overlooked a now disused graveyard of Little St. Mary's Church. Second, they gave easy access to the outside of the college. In those days, there were strict curfews for undergraduates. After a designated hour, the gates to the college were locked. Students trying to get in or out of the college after curfew would often climb through the windows. So the school authorities had put heavy metal bars across all the windows, which gave the rooms a rather prisonlike atmosphere.

But Grimes insisted that neither the graveyard, nor the bars, bothered him in the slightest. A true scholar, he said, should not be distracted by his surroundings.

One morning, Seth and another student named Jackson were sitting in one of the college common rooms reading, when Peter Grimes came in. He looked terrible. His face was white and there were dark circles under his sunken eyes. Seth assumed that he either was ill or had been up all night.

"Are you all right?" asked Seth. "You look as if you haven't slept all night."

"I haven't," Grimes replied.

"Working on an essay?"

"No," he said.

Seth was curious, but he didn't know Grimes that well, and didn't want to pry. After a few moments of hesitation, Grimes continued. "No. As a matter of fact, this is the third time it's happened in the last ten days."

"What has happened?"

"I've been kept awake by something scratching on the windows," he said.

"All night?"

"That's what it amounts to," said Grimes. "I go to bed soon after eleven. I read for a short while, then I fall asleep. After about an hour or so, this scratching noise wakes me up. As soon as I turn on the light and go to see what it is, it stops, so I go back to bed and go to sleep, and I haven't been asleep long when I'm wakened again by the same noise. When this has happened two or three times, I can't get off to sleep again, and I lie twisting and turning until morning."

Grimes said that there were no trees or bushes near enough to the window for branches rubbing against the glass to account for the scratching. Besides, as soon as he got up and went to the window, the noise stopped until he went back to bed. He thought that it might be someone playing a practical joke on him.

"Could be, I suppose," replied Seth.

Jackson, the third student in the room, had been listening to the conversation, and suddenly he joined in. "No. It'll be the vampire."

"What do you mean, vampire?" Grimes asked. "Do you mean bats?"

"No, I mean vampire," Jackson said. "Little St.

Mary's churchyard reputedly houses a vampire. The only one in England and, I believe I'm right in saying, one of just seven still active in Europe."

Grimes was incredulous. "You don't really believe in that sort of nonsense, do you?"

"Perhaps," said Jackson. "I know that nothing on earth would persuade me to have your rooms, Grimes. Good morning."

And with those words he left.

When he had gone, Grimes turned to Seth. "You don't believe in vampires, do you?"

"I've not given it any serious thought. I didn't even know they are supposed to exist, out of the pages of Bram Stoker."

It turned out that Grimes had given the matter serious thought. He knew a great deal about the vampire traditions in England and elsewhere. But he insisted that he did not believe in vampires, and still believed that some of the boys from the town, or perhaps some of the other students, were playing a joke on him.

The story of the vampire got around the college, and Grimes took a good deal of kidding about it, which he did not appreciate. He was particularly angry at a fellow called Chapman, who was giving him an exceptionally hard time.

But when more than a week passed and no

more scratching noises were heard, interest in the vampire died down, and Seth almost forgot about his conversation with Grimes. Then he heard from another friend that Grimes had been rushed to the infirmary in the middle of the night.

"What's wrong with him?"

"Bit of a mystery. Some of the chaps on his floor heard a scream come from his rooms, rushed down and found him collapsed and gibbering on the floor. One of his windows was open. One of his wrists seems to have been scraped raw. They sent for the Dean, and the Dean called the ambulance."

The college authorities took a very serious view of the incident. They conducted a careful investigation. The paint on the outside of the window overlooking the churchyard had been badly scratched. Yet there were no footprints in the soft earth beneath the window. The college was divided into two camps, those for and those against the vampire theory.

Grimes himself was in severe shock and it was several days before Seth was able to visit him.

"I'm sorry to hear about your accident," Seth said.

"It wasn't any accident."

Grimes then explained what had happened to

him. He had gone to bed as usual around eleven, and had been asleep for a short time when the scratchings began again. This time they didn't stop when he switched on the light.

"I was feeling particularly peeved when I got out of bed, because I was very tired and knew from what had happened before that I probably wouldn't get to sleep again.

"The noise was coming from one of the sitting-room windows, so I made my way there. As I went into the room, the scratching grew louder and increased in speed. It was as if whoever was there was getting more and more excited as I came nearer."

Grimes peered outside and could just make out a hooded figure moving up and down next to the window, drumming its fingers on the glass. "My immediate thought was that it was some silly ass dressed up and trying to frighten me. I shouted to him to go away, and that I would call the porter if he didn't stop fooling around."

That just seemed to make matters worse. The figure then began hitting the glass so hard that it seemed as if he would break it. Then Grimes did something that he could not account for. "I only realized what I was doing when my hand was actually on the window-catch. I tried to draw it back, but couldn't. Without any willing from me, my hand began to loosen the catch . . . As the catch came off, he lurched at the window, which flew open, catching me on the forehead." He pointed to a bandage on his right temple. "He lunged against the bars with such force, I swear they shook, and he thrust an arm through the window and seized hold of my right wrist.

"I tried to pull his fingers off my hand, and as I did so noticed how long they were and that they did not look like fingers at all, but an eagle's talons. The pain in my wrist was awful."

During the struggle the figure's hood fell back. "What I saw made me panic. I renewed my struggle to get free from his grip, and when I realized I couldn't, I let out a shriek and passed out. I don't remember any more until I came round in this bed."

When Grimes tried to describe the face that he had seen, he apologized because he could only come up with cliches: eyes like burning coals and fangs. The classical description of a vampire.

"Could it have been a mask?"

"No."

Grimes took his right hand out from under the bed covers. The flesh around the wrist was still raw, and there were four distinct scars that could have been made by sharp and abnormally long fingernails.

Of course, it could all have been an elaborate and cruel practical joke. But Grimes could never be convinced of that. He took a term off from school, and would never return to his old rooms at the college. They were taken by a very down-to-earth mathematician. When he was asked if he heard any scratchings on his windows, he would answer with a smile, "From time to time, but they don't worry me. I had heavy new shutters fitted on the inside."

It was nearly a year before the marks on Grimes' wrist disappeared. The experience also seemed to have changed him. From that point on, he was more nervous and withdrawn than ever.

8

The Highgate Vampire

"The tomb in the day-time, and when wreathed with fresh flowers, had looked grim and gruesome enough; but now, some days afterwards, when the flowers hung lank and dead, their whites turning to rust and their greens to browns; when the spider and the beetle had resumed their accustomed dominance; when time-discolored stone, and dust-encrusted mortar, and rusty dank iron and tarnished brass, and clouded silver-plating gave back the feeble glimmer of a candle, the effect was more miserable and sordid than could have been imagined. It conveyed irresistibly the idea that life

—animal life—was not the only thing which could pass away."

That is how Dr. Seward describes the tomb of the unfortunate Lucy Westenra in Bram Stoker's *Dracula*. Lucy had died under mysterious circumstances, and had been placed in the family tomb in a London graveyard. Within a few days of the entombment, however, disturbing stories begin appearing in the newspapers. Several small children living in the neighborhood of the cemetery disappear. They are found the next morning. They say that they have been taken for a walk by a "bloofer lady"—babytalk for "beautiful lady." The children all appear to have slight wounds on their necks.

The police think that a rat or a dog has caused the wounds, but the learned Professor Van Helsing knows better. His worst fears have been confirmed. Lucy is not dead. Dracula has turned her into one of the undead. She has become a vampire! At night she leaves her tomb to find victims whose blood she can drink.

Van Helsing and his companions break into the crypt at night and find Lucy's coffin empty. The logical Dr. Seward says the body must have been stolen by tomb robbers, but Professor Van Helsing brushes such a mundane objection aside. He says that Lucy Westenra is out in search of victims. Van

Helsing and Seward set up a vigil to watch the tomb, and Seward catches a glimpse of a white figure moving through the graveyard.

"I had to go round headstones and railed-off tombs, and I stumbled over graves. The sky was overcast, and somewhere far off an early cock crew. A little way off, beyond a line of scattered juniper-trees, which marked the pathway to the church, a white dim figure flitted in the direction of the tomb. The tomb itself was hidden by trees, and I could not see where the figure disappeared."

Professor Van Helsing and his companions return during the daytime, when the vampire must sleep in its coffin and is therefore less dangerous to the living. They have with them "a round wooden stake, some two and a half or three inches thick and about three feet long. One end of it was hardened by charring in the fire, and was sharpened to a fine point." They also have a heavy hammer, and are determined to finally dispatch the undead, by driving a stake through her heart.

"The Thing in the coffin writhed; and a hideous, blood-curdling screech came from the opened red lips. The body shook and quivered and twisted in wild contortions; the sharp white teeth champed together till the lips were cut, and the mouth was smeared with a crimson foam."

It is one of the most memorable and terrifying scenes in the entire novel.

Dracula fanatics, who have tried to trace every possible reference in the Stoker novel, have long speculated over which of London's many cemeteries contained the Westenra family tomb that was the setting for these terrible events. Stoker is not very helpful. He wrote vaguely of a cemetery near Hampstead Heath. He also says that when Professor Van Helsing and his companions first tried to find the graveyard, there was "quite a mix-up as to locality." But most of those who are familiar with Victorian London, in which much of *Dracula* was set, are convinced that Stoker used as his model Highgate Cemetery.

Highgate Cemetery was built in the nineteenth century and by the 1880s, the time of Dracula, was one of the most fashionable burying places in London. Actually, it was in the village of Highgate, just outside of London, but it has long since been incorporated into the metropolis. Highgate Cemetery was, and is, a gloomy, gothic monument to the Victorian cult of death. The older part of the crowded cemetery is stuffed with weeping marble angels, massive mausoleums, even a place called the Terrace Catacombs. It is just exactly the sort of place where one might imagine that Lucy Westenra was buried, and it may well have been in Bram Stoker's mind when he wrote *Dracula*.

Actually, a lot of famous people are buried in Highgate. The scientist Michael Faraday and the writer George Eliot are there; so are the wife and daughter of Charles Dickens. Karl Marx, the philosophical father of communism, is entombed beneath an imposing monument which was once a place of pilgrimage for Communists from all parts of the world. But now it is Dracula that draws the crowds.

Guides who conduct tours of the cemetery are used to being asked where Dracula's grave is. And they are used to the visitors' disappointment when told that it isn't there.

It seems that whenever a movie or TV company is shooting a vampire story, they turn up at Highgate to film the weathered crosses and vine-encrusted crypts as background. If you're a devotee of vampire films, you've seen Highgate Cemetery many times, even though you may not be aware of it. The private group that maintains the old cemetery now charges a large fee for filming inside its gates. "Dracula is big business," says one of the guides.

But the vampire association has not always been a happy or profitable one for Highgate. It may have cost more than it ever made, for not so very long ago the old cemetery was literally over-run with vandals and vampire hunters—sometimes it was hard to tell the difference between the two —attracted by tales of a real modern vampire.

By the end of World War II, Highgate had fallen out of favor as a burial place, and the older parts of it were so unkept and overgrown that they were not only difficult, but actually dangerous, to walk through. An unwary visitor risked falling into a deep hole, created when one of the underground vaults collapsed. The cemetery had become a vir-tual wilderness and home for a thriving population of foxes, rats, and hedgehogs. There were the usual stories of ghosts and secret ceremonies held among the crumbling tombstones—the sort of stories that are told about every old cemetery.

Then, in the late 1960s, stories of a more un-usual nature began to circulate. They first appeared in local newspapers. There was an eerie similarity to the way Professor Van Helsing first learned of the nightly roving of the vampire that Lucy Wes-tenra had become. There were no children taken for nightly walks by a mysterious "bloofer lady," but there were a couple of teenaged girls who were passing the north gate of the cemetery when they had a vision of corpses rising from open graves. One of the girls, Elizabeth Wojdyla, began having nightmares in which a ghastly figure with a corpselike face appeared at her bedroom window. She became pale and began losing weight. She went to the doctors, but no one seemed to know what was wrong with her. It all sounded very like the afflictions reported by Lucy Westenra, once she became Dracula's victim.

Others passing the cemetery reported seeing a strange corpselike figure staring at them from inside the gates. One young man insisted that he had actually been knocked down by the thing. A number of dead animals, mostly foxes, were found on the cemetery grounds with all the blood drained from their bodies. Skeptics said that the animals had been killed by the caretaker's dog, and the blood had been drained from them when the dog dragged the remains around. But many were not satisfied by such a mundane explanation. To them, there was only one cause: A vampire had risen from its Highgate grave!

Now as you might well imagine, all of this excitement attracted some strange characters to the old cemetery. One of the oddest was a fellow by the name of Sean Manchester. On some occasions he had called himself Ruthwen Glenavon and George Byron. Manchester is sort of a free-lance occultist and founder of the Vampire Research Society and the International Society for the Advancement of Irreproducible Vampire and Lycanthropy Research

(ISAIVLR). He has adopted the title of Reverend Manchester and says he is a lay priest of the Celtic Catholic Church. In addition, he is a direct descendent of the poet Lord Byron, and he grew up in Robin Hood's Sherwood Forest, or so he has claimed.

Manchester says that he met Wojdyla and cured her, where doctors had failed, by hanging garlic around her room, giving her a silver cross to wear, and generally following the Van Helsing formula for getting rid of the unwanted attentions of a vampire. Then Manchester decided that he would track the monster to its lair.

On March 13, 1970, a Friday naturally, Sean Manchester led a crowd of about a hundred people to a burial vault that he suspected contained the vampire. Manchester and a couple of assistants got into the tomb through a hole in the roof. They found three empty coffins, and "purified" the area with a ritual that used garlic, salt, holy water, and all the usual vampire repellants.

It didn't work. The press continued to report sightings of a corpselike figure in the vicinity of Highgate Cemetery. All of the attention was attracting vandals, who were doing a tremendous amount of damage to the monuments. Someone actually dug up a corpse and tried to burn it.

Manchester decided that the vampire must have

moved to a new location. In August, 1970, he went back and found another likely looking tomb. This one seemed to have an extra coffin in it. This, he decided, was the vampire's new resting place. And since it was daytime, the vampire must be asleep in its coffin.

Sean Manchester told the story of what happened next many times. Each time it seemed to get better, more vivid, more ghastly. Here was a 1985 version from his book, *The Highgate Vampire*:

"My torch lit up in unnerving revelation the sleeping form of something that had long been dead; something nevertheless gorged and stinking with the life-blood of others, fresh clots of which still adhered to the edge of the mouth whose fetid breath made me sick to my stomach. The glazed eyes stared horribly—almost mocking me, almost knowing that my efforts to destroy it would be thwarted. Under the parchment-like skin a faint bluish tinge could be detected. The face was the color and appearance of a three-day-old corpse."

Just as Manchester was ready to drive a stake through the heart of the monster, one of his assistants reminded him that this would be desecration of a corpse, and therefore an illegal act. A little technicality like that would not have bothered Professor Van Helsing. But Sean Manchester didn't want any trouble with the law. He put away his stake and hammer, and repeated the whole garlic and holy water ritual. Later, he said that he had the door to the vault sealed with cement into which garlic had been mixed.

The ritual wasn't any more effective than it had been the first time. Manchester chased the thing for another three years. In the winter of 1973, he read an article in a London paper about a deserted nineteenth-century mansion in north London that the local people had dubbed "the House of Dracula." Proof enough! Manchester and a couple of assistants rushed to the scene. They broke into the house one afternoon and found the undead thing resting in an enormous black casket in the basement. It looked even worse than it had before.

"Burning, fierce eyes beneath black furrowed brows stared with hellish reflection. Yellow at the edges with blood-red centers, they were unlike any other beast of prey. Flared nostrils connected to a thin, high-bridged nose. The mouth still set in its cruel expression, with lips drawn far back, as if unable to contain the fangs."

There were to be no scruples about desecrating a corpse this time. Manchester grabbed for his stake and hammer and "with a mighty blow" drove it right into the creature's chest. There was a roar "from the bowels of hell" and the creature just collapsed and melted into a puddle of brown slime at the bottom of the casket.

Manchester and his associates burned the remains. Later, the house was torn down and the site used for public housing for the elderly. There have been no complaints of vampires from the residents.

Gaudy as Sean Manchester was, he was a model of decorum when compared to another vampire hunter who was attracted by the tales of undead doings at Highgate Cemetery. He was David Farrant. Farrant was a young man who lived in the area and worked as a hospital orderly. He said he had seen the vampire during his own nightly forays into Highgate. He described the monster as being eight feet tall.

Farrant had jumped the cemetery walls so many times that some suspected that *he* was the Highgate vampire. In 1971, Farrant was arrested for trespassing, not once but several times. At one trial the judge dismissed the charges, but advised the would-be vampire hunter to see a doctor.

That didn't discourage Farrant one little bit. He

kept just coming back, and his claims became more and more grandiose. He said that he was head of a nationwide organization dedicated to driving stakes through the hearts of vampires. Armed with stake and hammer, he led TV reporters on tours of suspected vampire lairs in Highgate. The police believed that Farrant and his friends were conducting black magic rituals inside of some of the tombs. He was arrested again, this time on more serious charges, and put on trial in June, 1974, in what the press dubbed "The Nude Rituals Case." As you might imagine, the British tabloids, which have never been noted for their good taste or accuracy, loved this, and covered the case in every juicy detail.

One of the odder charges was that Farrant had sent what the English call poppets, or what we might call voodoo dolls, stuck full of pins to a couple of the detectives who were scheduled to testify against him. They were apparently intended as a warning.

As far as satanic and nude rituals, Farrant said that the satanic rites had been performed by others. The nude ritual, he said, was part of an exorcism to drive away the evil forces. The defense didn't go down too well. Farrant was convicted on a variety of charges and sentenced to four years and eight months in jail, plus a hefty fine. He was paroled in 1976, after serving two years of his sentence.

David Farrant then went back to, dare I say, his old haunts. He went around claiming that he was a "high priest" in Sean Manchester's organization. Manchester disavowed any connection. This irritated Farrant, who challenged Manchester to a duel. But it never took place. And finally even the tabloids lost interest.

Though all of these occult goings-on may have fascinated and titillated the British public, and readers of American supermarket tabloids as well, the guardians of Highgate Cemetery were not amused. The damage to the cemetery had been extensive. Vaults were being broken into and corpses dragged out. In 1974, an architect, who made the mistake of parking near the cemetery one night, returned in the morning to find a headless corpse in his car.

At great expense, the cemetery fences were repaired. The gates to some of the older sections were locked to all who did not go on a tour or possess a special permit. Volunteers cleaned the paths and hacked away some of the excess plant life that had grown up over the last hundred years or so. They were careful not to clean it up too much, however, and destroy its famous atmosphere of "Victorian gloom."

The cemetery keepers have tried to discourage all the vampire rumors. They even prevailed upon a nearby gift shop to stop selling Manchester's book about his adventures at Highgate. But the questions about Dracula's grave keep coming anyway.

It is quite impossible to wander the narrow paths of Highgate, even in the middle of the day, past the crumbling stone crosses, and marble angels, the vine-encrusted crypts and mausoleums which are familiar to you from dozens of half-remembered films, and not feel that this is indeed Dracula's lair. And if the vampire is not here, he surely should be.

SELECTED BIBLIOGRAPHY

Aylesworth, Thomas G. *The Story of Vampires.* New York: McGraw-Hill, 1977.

Cohen, Daniel. *A Natural History of Unnatural Things.* New York: The McCall Publishing Co., 1971.

Dalby, Richard. *Dracula's Brood.* New York: Dorset, 1987.

Editors of Time-Life Books. Enchanted World Series. *Night Creatures.* Arlington, VA: Time-Life Books, 1985.

Farson, Daniel. *Vampires, Zombies and Monster Men.* New York, Doubleday, 1976.

Florescu, Radu and Raymond T. McNally. *Dracula: A Biography of Vlad the Impaler, 1431-1476.* New York: Hawthorn Books, 1973.

Garden, Nancy. *Vampires.* Philadelphia: Lippincott, 1973.

Glut, Donald. *True Vampires of History*. New York: H.C. Publishers, 1971.

Guiley, Rosemary Ellen. *Vampires Among Us*. New York: Pocket Books, 1991.

Hill, Douglas. *The History of Ghosts, Vampires and Werewolves*. New York: Harper, 1973.

Hoyt, Olga. *Lust for Blood*. New York: Stein and Day, 1984.

Masters, Anthony. *The Natural History of the Vampire*. New York: Putnam's, 1972.

McNally, Raymond T. *A Clutch of Vampires*. Greenwich, CT: New York Graphic Society, 1974.

———and Radu Florescu. *In Search of Dracula*. New York, Warner Books, 1973.

Rymer, James Malcolm (?). *Varney the Vampire*. 2 vols. First published 1847. New York: Dover edition, 1972.

Rice, Anne. *Interview With a Vampire*. New York: Knopf, 1976.

Summers, Montagu. *The Vampire in Europe*. New Hyde Park, N.Y.: University Books, n.d.

———. *The Vampire His Kith and Kin*. New Hyde Park, N.Y.: University Books, 1960.

Underwood, Peter. *The Vampire's Bedside Companion*. London: Leslie Frowin, 1975.

Wright, Dudley. *The Book of Vampires*. First published 1914. New York: Causeway edition, 1973.

Wolf, Leonard. *The Annotated Dracula*. New York: Clarkson N. Potter, 1975.

———. *A Dream of Dracula: In Search of the Living Dead*. Boston, Little Brown, 1972.

DANIEL COHEN is the author of over 150 nonfiction books for adults and young readers on subjects ranging from ghosts and dinosaurs to monsters and the supernatural. He is known as an authority on ghosts, and titles include *Great Ghosts, Railway Ghosts and Highway Horrors, Ghost in the House, Young Ghosts.*

Mr. Cohen is a native of Chicago and former managing editor of *Science Digest* magazine. He and his wife, Susan, who is also a writer, have collaborated on a number of books and recently researched and wrote *Where to Find Dinosaurs Today.* They also wrote *What Kind of Dog Is That?* and their interest in Clumber Spaniels resulted in the first chapter of *Real Vampires.*

The Cohens live in Cape May Court House, New Jersey.